THE OFFICIAL BOOK

First published in 1998 by
Virgin Books
an imprint of
**Virgin Publishing Ltd
Thames Wharf Studios
Rainville Road
London W6 9HT**

Copyright © Aqua 1998

This book is sold subject to the condition that it shall not, by way of trade or otherwise, be lent, resold, hired out or otherwise circulated without the publisher's prior written consent in any form or binding other than that in which it is published and without a similar condition being imposed upon the subsequent purchaser.

A catalogue record for this book is available from the British Library

ISBN 07535 0224 0

Printed and bound in Great Britain by
Butler & Tanner Ltd, Frome and London

Colour reproduction:
Colourwise ltd

Designed by
Jon Lucas, Ad Vantage
The Old School House
66 Leonard Street
London EC2A 4LT

Manager of **Aqua**: and Merchandise Contact
John Aagaard, TG Management
Tel: +45 98 16 87 44
Fax: +45 98 13 59 44
e-mail: tgm-hq@post3.tele.dk

Picture Credits
Ray Burmiston: 1, 3, 32, 33, 41, 45, 47, 51
Robin Skjoldborg: 7,8, 9, 13, 14, 15, 25, 31, 34, 35, 36, 37, 39, 46, 49, 55, 64
Aqua: 10, 11, 28, 29, 42, 43, 56, 57
Alex Futtrup: 16, 18, 19, 20, 21, 22, 27, 38, 61
Niclas Anker: 1, 14, 17, 23
René Schütze: 59
Anders Sørensen: 60

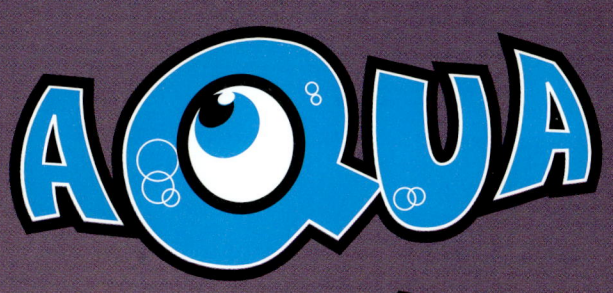

THE OFFICIAL BOOK

JACQUI SWIFT

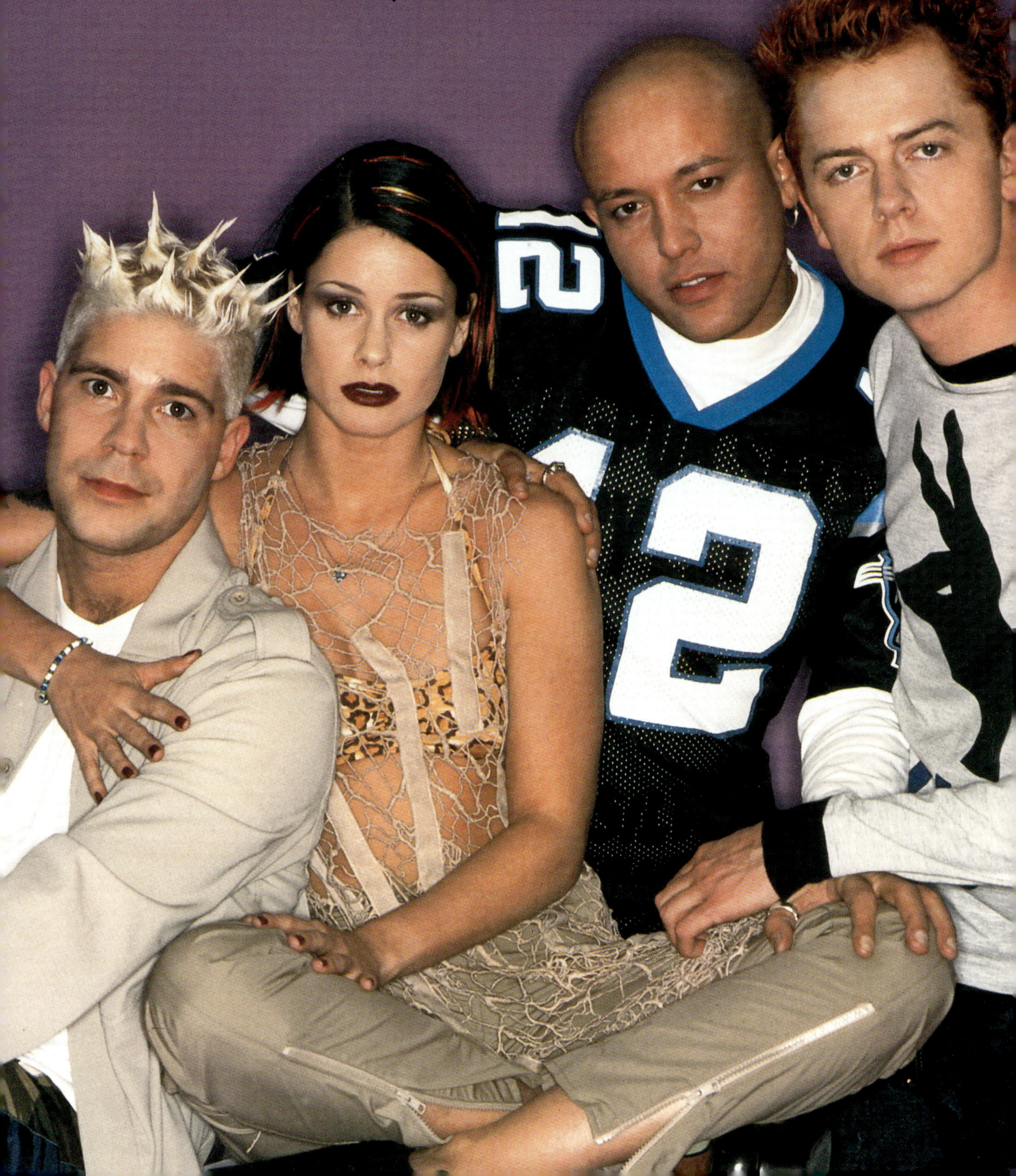

'We're serious but we don't take ourselves that seriously. We're perfectionists and we know what we're doing. We see ourselves as a happy and fun band. You can get what you want to get out of the band. Basically it's all about having fun, being yourself.'

RENÉ
MAY 1998

CONTENTS

THE AQUA STORY:
  SCENE ONE: THE EARLY DAYS 6
RENÉ 10
THE AQUA STORY:
  SCENE TWO: ENTER LENE 12
AROUND THE WORLD 16
THE AQUA STORY:
  SCENE THREE: NEW NAME, NEW LOOK 24
CLAUS 28
THE AQUA STORY:
  SCENE FOUR: ROSES AND RECORDS 30
AQUA STYLE 34
THE AQUA STORY:
  SCENE FIVE: CALL BARBIE A DOCTOR! 40
SØREN 42
THE AQUA STORY:
  SCENE SIX: TURN TO A DIFFERENT STYLE 44
1,2,3 ACTION! 48
THE AQUA STORY:
  SCENE SEVEN: THE FUTURE IS AQUA 50
LENE 56
AQUA LIVE 58
AQUA FACTS 62
ACKNOWLEDGEMENTS 64

THE AQUA STORY: SCENE ONE

THE EARLY DAYS

Something special exploded onto the worldwide music scene in 1997, something unique, something fresh and something that could never be duplicated. That something was Aqua – Lene Nystrøm, René Dif, Søren Rasted and Claus Norreen. Four like-minded performers with the desire, commitment and talent to be big!

The ingredients that would eventually become Aqua first started to come together in Denmark at the end of 1994, when René met two aspiring musicians, Søren and Claus. René had made his name as a DJ, working on radio and TV stations throughout Scandinavia. He grew up listening to the sounds of Hip-Hop artists like The Rocksteady Crew and Grandmaster Flash, which helped him to develop another talent as well as his disc-spinning ability: he could rap!

'I remember when The Rocksteady Crew were playing in Copenhagen,' he recalls, 'It was so funny – we were running down the streets as fast as we could. We HAD to see them.'

Claus Norreen was a gifted chemical engineering student, working part-time at a gas station to earn some spare cash, when he befriended a young man called Søren Rasted. They immediately found that they shared a passion for music.

Claus had already been in numerous school bands, playing keyboards and making industrial techno sounds. Growing up, he had idolized New Wave bands like Depeche Mode, Kraftwerk and the Human League. As a child he was fascinated by electronics and remembers sitting for hours putting his father's old radio together.

SCENE ONE: THE EARLY DAYS

'Even before Søren and I met we had the same ideas – we wanted to make our own type of music, our own stuff.'
CLAUS

At school, his hobby developed into a talent when he bought a basic keyboard. When he was 14 he bought his first synthesizer, developing his skills even further.

Claus remembers: 'I couldn't really play and had to learn. I was just copying songs I liked with a friend. That was the start of it all.'

Søren, on the other hand, had been taught the piano from the age of five by his mother, who had passed her musical ability on to him. Søren kept his interest in music when he visited the USA as an exchange student, staying with a musical family.

Claus and Søren realized that though they had different musical tastes and influences (Søren was into The The and Simple Minds) both were keen on experimenting

and composing tunes, so one day they decided to play together.

'Even before Søren and I met we had the same ideas – we wanted to make our own type of music, our own stuff.' says Claus.

The duo set to work writing and playing tunes, and one day they ran into René. Søren and Claus had won a small competition to write the soundtrack for a children's film in 1994. For one of the tracks they needed a rapper, and who did they turn to...? René!

It was 1994 and the foundations of the band were in place. The trio became firm friends and began writing together, although they all agreed that something was lacking – a talented female singer. It was René's job to find the right girl – would they ever find her?

> 'I couldn't really play and had to learn. I was just copying songs I liked with a friend. That was the start of it all.'
> **CLAUS**

NAME	René Dif
NICKNAME	Dif, Pâsan, Diffedrengen
BIRTHPLACE	Frederiksberg, Denmark
DATE OF BIRTH	17 October 1967
EYE COLOUR	Brown
HAIR COLOUR	What hair?
HEIGHT	6ft 3in/187cm
WEIGHT	14st/89kg
PARENTS' PROFESSION	Both work at a hospital
LIVES	Copenhagen/London
DISTINGUISHING FEATURES	Scars on his face from a dog bite, tattoo on left shoulder
FAVOURITE FOOD	Sushi and hot Mexican
FAVOURITE MOVIE	Moon Base Alpha
FAVOURITE TV SHOW	Ricki Lake and David Letterman
FAVOURITE POSSESSIONS	His clothes and his CDs
FAVOURITE CLOTHES	Lots of colour and a kilt with nothing underneath
BEST EXPERIENCE	When his daughter was born
WORST EXPERIENCE	Having his appendix removed
GREATEST STRENGTH	His cheerful enthusiasm
GREATEST WEAKNESS	Bad phone manners
EDUCATION	PhD in this and that!
FORMER JOBS	DJ in Scandinavia and Southern Europe
BEST TIME OF HIS CAREER	Whenever people are positive about Aqua
HEROES AND ROLE MODELS	None

THE AQUA STORY: SCENE TWO

ENTER LENE

Lene Nyström was born in Norway's oldest city of Tønsberg in 1973. A live wire as a child, she began to perform at the age of ten, although she had been taking jazz ballet classes since she was six!

Lene grew up listening to Elvis, The Rolling Stones and – like any Scandinavian youngster – Abba. However, it was the Norwegian Eurovision winner Bobbysocks that first inspired the young Lene to perform.

She explains: 'When I was about 11 or 12, me and my best friends would copy Bobbysocks in our pink and black outfits. One day I was standing in the living room, performing in front of my family and my elder sister, when suddenly my sister punched me in my stomach! It was this that made me realize that I had to use my whole body to sing. Before that I had been singing flat.'

While Abba and Bobbysocks provided the inspiration for Miss Nyström's music, her unlikely dancing inspiration was an English pop star called... Shakin' Stevens! Lene laughs as she recalls dancing around to the records of this British rock'n'roller, who for many was a pale imitation of Elvis Presley. This infatuation soon waned as she fell in love with other artists including Michael Jackson and Pink Floyd, all of whom would be influential in her role as singer with the mighty Aqua.

Lene had already had a big chance to show off her vocal skills when, while hosting a Scandinavian TV game show, she was thrown in front of the cameras to sing the Randy Crawford song 'Almaz', accompanied only by a piano. A star was born.

'I had a really great time and learned a lot on that TV show,' she says. The producers were impressed with the budding star – so impressed that Lene and the TV host went to work on a cruise ship, sailing between Copenhagen in Denmark and Oslo in Norway. It was on the ship that Lene first encountered a certain René Dif.

René was working as a DJ on board the ship and searching for a singer. Little did he know, when he met Lene, that she was the one he was looking for – René had fallen in love with the beautiful Lene without knowing that she could sing!

SCENE TWO: ENTER LENE

Lene remembers: 'He was playing me some music from another project he'd worked on. I remember listening to another girl singing it and thinking "I can sing better than her." I told René and his reaction was "Can you sing?" That was it – I was in the band!'

When René proudly showed Claus and Søren a video of Lene singing they were equally thrilled and so they invited her over to Denmark. Lene met up with Claus and Søren and they just clicked. The foursome spent the whole weekend together at Søren's parents' house – just the four of them and a piano.

The early days were simply fun. Claus, Søren, René and Lene hung out together, getting to know each other and just dabbling with the odd tune.

'It was so important that we got on,' explains René, 'or it wouldn't work.'

For the next six months, Lene travelled back and forth between her native Norway and her adopted Denmark, spending as much time with the band as she could while holding down her job at a jewellers.

As work commitments intensified, Lene was forced to quit her job, relying on René to help her get by.

'It sounds funny now,' laughs René, 'but we really lived on nothing. I was DJ-ing at the weekends and that was it.'

The four were starting to take things a bit more seriously. They began to buckle down, and as time went by, they worked later and later, spending up to 14 hours in Claus's flat working on their music.

As is the case with many bands at the start of their career, times were hard for the four friends, but they helped each other out and there was never any talk of quitting. There were difficult times, times at which Lene admits to having been a touch restless.

'When you're 20, you want to do everything at once. You don't have the patience to sit down and wait. The boys just held me back and said: "Everything's going to be all right, just take your time."'

> 'It sounds funny now,' laughs René, 'but we really lived on nothing. I was DJ-ing at the weekends and that was it.'
> RENÉ

AROUND THE

Their international fame has given Aqua the chance to travel the world, visiting all the countries that have contributed to their success.

On their 18-month-long tour, they visited over 26 countries including Korea, Hong Kong and Japan. They thrilled audiences all over the world, and played in Denmark in front of 20,000 people at the Skanderborg Festival.

'We were looking forward to the tour so much. It was part of the whole dream for us, being able to make music and travel!' explains Claus. To the band, Japan was like a mini-holiday and they were all very, very excited. They worked from early morning to late at night having their pictures taken and meeting as many people as possible. Whenever they had any time off they spent it getting to know the people helping to promote them in Asia.

'The people were so nice,' exclaims Lene. 'We'd never seen people that polite before.'

'We were looking forward to the tour so much. It was part of the whole dream for us, being able to make music and travel!'
CLAUS

WORLD

AROUND THE WORLD

'Also, whenever we went to a radio station everyone who was dealing with Aqua at the record company came along, which wouldn't happen elsewhere. It was like a parade with a sign saying "Aqua are coming!" '

In Japan, Aqua started off in Osaka before moving on to Tokyo. They went everywhere, including places where pop bands don't usually go. A normal day would include a minimum of 14 interviews and photo sessions!

While they were in Tokyo, one fantastic experience for Lene, René, Claus and Søren was playing baseball at The Tokyo Dome. The arena was packed with Aqua fans, all chanting and cheering when they caught a glimpse of their heroes.

'It was such a big thing!' boasts Lene 'and such an honour to play baseball there. The fans were so loud – they were screaming continuously. We couldn't believe it

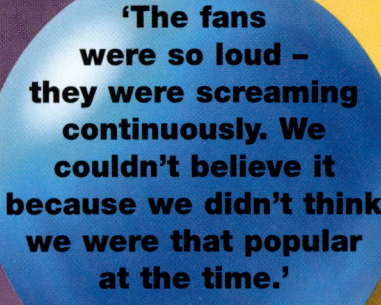

'The fans were so loud – they were screaming continuously. We couldn't believe it because we didn't think we were that popular at the time.'
LENE

because we didn't think we were that popular at the time.'

If it came as a surprise to the band how popular they were in Tokyo, then it must have dawned on them by the time they reached Nagoya.

'We played a club in Nagoya,' explains Claus 'and it was just a mad flip out. We arrived and there was water running down the walls because there were so many people there.'

AROUND THE WORLD

The eager fans had been waiting and waiting to see pop's newest sensation play. Ever-patient, the fans began to sing Aqua's songs in their excitement!

'I think they'd even invented their own version of 'Roses are Red', making up the words as they went along,' laughs Søren. 'We were saying to each other "What are they singing?"'

Aqua have fond memories of so many of the places they visited. Whether it was playing to 15 people or 250,000 as they did in Spain, each event was special for different reasons.

'I remember a club we did in Bangkok,' says Claus. 'We were going to the venue in the car and we were stuck in this traffic jam. We were all wondering what the delay was for, until we realized that we were stuck in the jam to go to our own show!'

Another highlight was hearing the news that 'Barbie Girl' had gone into the American Billboard 100 at number seven, a record for a new band.

'That was wonderful,' exclaims Lene. 'We were in Malaysia when the news came through and we all jumped, screaming, into the air!'

> 'We were in Malaysia when the news came through and we all jumped, screaming, into the air!'
> **LENE**

In Los Angeles in September 1997 they were treated to a special Aqua party, arriving in a stretch limousine to celebrate *Aquarium* achieving gold album status! During their visit they played their first US performance to a wild audience at the Radio Jammin' 92.3 show. Afterwards they went bowling with Z100 New York and got stuck in an elevator for half an hour before the show! They also appeared on the Ricki Lake TV show, before heading off to France and The Netherlands, where they received yet more discs and appeared in front of 18,000 people at The Pepsi Pop Show in Rotterdam.

Aqua were a household name now. Aquamania was everywhere!

AROUND THE WORLD

In April 1998 Aqua wowed 17,000 fans in Sydney, Australia. It was hard to believe that exactly a year ago they had performed to only 86 people in Holbæck, Denmark!

With the constant attention surrounding the four band members, you'd think it would be scary at times, but they are surrounded by people all the time, people they know, have faith and believe in.

'We know nothing will go wrong with these people around,' adds a trusting Søren. The band admit that they still have to pinch themselves sometimes when they realize how quickly they have gained worldwide fame.

'It's weird to think that just about wherever you are in the

> 'It's weird to think that just about wherever you are in the world everyone knows your name.'
> RENÉ

22

world everyone knows your name,' explains René. 'We were sitting in a café in Soho in London once, just drinking our coffee, and people were walking by saying "Hi René!" That's the weirdest!'

Their 18-month tour came to an end in February 1998 in New Zealand. In Auckland, over 200 police had to close the main street because more than 25,000 people had come to see Aqua. This was the largest crowd the city had seen since the last Americas Cup! When all the fuss had died down, the band treated themselves to a little memento. Each had a special tattoo: Søren on his left shoulder, René on the back of his neck, Claus on his left shoulder and Lene in the small of her back. Tattoos that would remain forever, just as the name, sound and style of Aqua will be around forever!

THE AQUA STORY: SCENE THREE

NEW NAME NEW LOOK

Before christening themselves Aqua, the band were known as Joyspeed and were signed to Warner Records.

Lene says: 'We thought "We've got a record contract now, so we're going to be world famous." We had a techno-type song called 'Itsy Bitsy Spider' and they didn't really promote it. We never even used to meet the people we were working with! We wanted out and cancelled the contract.'

The band, now out of the record contract they'd wanted so badly, didn't despair. After a while, and a lot of negotiation, they signed a new deal with Universal Music Denmark in 1996. Their signing to Universal was clearly meant to happen: when the band had originally sent out demo tapes to record companies, the two which had shown an interest had been Universal and Warners!

They had all learned a lot about the music business and were ready to do things on their terms. They had always wanted to make Europop music and they would do it their way.

'Roses are Red', the debut single from the band, had actually been a side project and wasn't going to be a single release. They had made the record in a day, and had impressed Universal, who thought it was a poppy, clean number.

When they signed to Universal, the band had to find a new name to go with their new style.

SCENE THREE: NEW NAME NEW LOOK

'We were doing a concert in Copenhagen and we had to think of a name really quickly for the poster,' says Lene. 'René saw this poster for an aquarium and thought it would be a great name.' Of course, there were many other ideas before they arrived at the shorter version, Aqua, including the strange T-Bone Steak!

'We thought of so many names, but we kept saying "Oh no, not that!" 'laughs René. 'Then one night Søren and I were sitting in the studio and I just said "Well what about *Aquarium*?"'

The name was an obvious choice, a positive word fitting perfectly with the refreshing sound the band were beginning to make. It was genius, a new type of name which was unlike that of any other new band.

One person who believed in Aqua from the very start was Niclas Anker, the man who, in a way, Aqua consider to be the fifth member of the group. As Universal's Marketing Manager, he would advise the four on everything, and would help devise Aqua's unique style.

'Without him we wouldn't be who we are today. He never told us what to do, but he did say: "You can do it like this if you want, or go ahead with your own decision,"' explains René.

Another leading man in the Aqua story is manager John Aagaard. Niclas had suggested the band get together with John, who was already a well known manager in Denmark. When

> 'We were so eager that we signed and sent the contract back straight away! Then we partied our brains out!'
> **SØREN**

they met him they knew straight away that he was the man for them, although they didn't realize who he was at first!

They all went out for dinner with John, as it was very important for the band to get on with their manager from the start. 'It's like he's the father and we're his family!' remarks Lene.

The meal was a nerve-racking experience for Aqua; it was as if they were at a job interview, not knowing whether they'd got it or not! However, they all left the restaurant with a good feeling about the meeting, and a few weeks later John sent them a contract.

'We were so eager that we signed and sent it back straight away!' confesses Søren. 'Then we partied our brains out!"

Name	Claus Norreen
Nickname	Røde, Red, Rote, Claude
Birthplace	Charlottenlund, Denmark
Date of Birth	5 June 1970
Eye Colour	Green
Hair Colour	Red
Height	6ft 2in/187cm
Weight	11st 6lb/73kg
Parents' Profession	Hardworking pensioners
Lives	Copenhagen/London
Distinguishing Features	He's a meddling busybody
Favourite Food	All food
Favourite Movie	Bladerunner
Favourite TV Show	He's addicted to his remote control
Favourite Possession	His bank account
Favourite Clothes	Clean ones!
Best Experience	Too many to mention
Worst Experience	Losing family or friends
Greatest Strength	Patience
Greatest Weakness	Dark-haired girls
Education	High school
Former Jobs	Cleaning, gas station attendant, sales assistant in clothes store
Best Time of His Career	The first time the audience sang along at one of Aqua's shows
Heroes and Role Models	None

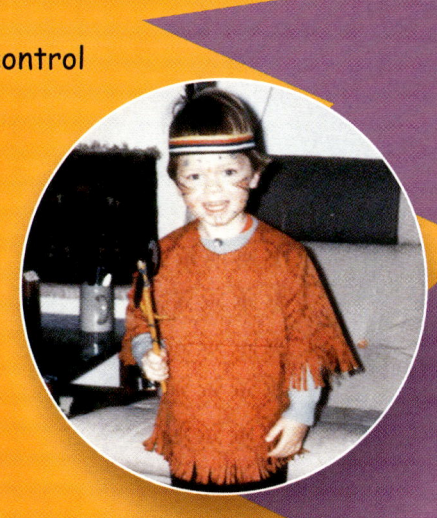

THE AQUA STORY: SCENE FOUR

ROSES AND RECORDS

When Aqua found out that 'Roses are Red' was to be the first single to be released under their new name and style, they decided to make a video that showed off their attitude and sense of fun. The band were so keen to make sure the video was just how they wanted it, they oversaw everything. They set up the whole thing themselves, even down to painting the blue screen background and buying all the props! Money was tight in the early days, but their luck was in. Sixty people, including some friends of Søren who made TV commercials, offered their services for free.

'We had only asked to borrow the filming gear for a day but they just said "We'll do it." It was great!' explains Søren. His parents were also on the set, making sandwiches and running around with the coffee, while the band were doing their own make-up and hair and cleaning up after themselves!

'We were very grateful to our friends,' says Claus. 'We showed what we were capable of, and proved to the company that we could give one hundred per cent.'

The band were so desperate to make the record a success that they became involved in everything. They would turn up at Universal's offices every day to help out, doing anything from packing CDs to phoning DJs to see if they were playing their new song.

> 'We showed what we were capable of, and proved to the company that we could give one hundred per cent.'
>
> CLAUS

SCENE FOUR: ROSES AND RECORDS

The response was incredible, as 'Roses are Red' went straight into the Danish charts at number 14, an amazing feat for a previously unknown band.

'We were dancing about when we heard,' laughs Claus, 'because for us it was as if we'd got to number one. I remember listening to Tjeklisten, which is one of the most important chart shows in Denmark because it's the listeners' chart. We were all sat there looking at each other, then they announced it and we went crazy, getting the champagne out to celebrate!'

The song reached number one and stayed there for nine weeks. Even when their next single 'My Oh My' was released, which stormed straight in at number one, 'Roses are Red' was still hanging in there!

'My Oh My' was released in Scandinavia and Asia too, hitting number one almost everywhere and proving that Aqua would definitely be around for a while.

It is often difficult for bands to follow up the success of a big

> 'We were all sat there looking at each other, then they announced it and we went crazy, getting the champagne out to celebrate!'
>
> **CLAUS**

hit single – but not for Aqua! Their popularity was growing from strength to strength.

The band spent the rest of 1996 locked away writing their debut album *Aquarium*, missing out on a summer on the beach with their friends. Released on 26 March 1997, *Aquarium* just kept selling and selling, remaining in the Danish Top 40 for a year and a half. Søren says: 'I think we only realized how successful the thing was after we'd come back from Asia, because while we'd been gone for so long all the papers had been writing about us.' The fascination from fans and the media was demonstrated by Aqua's nomination for a 1997 Danish Grammy, even though their record had only been out for a month!

'That was so way out!' claims René, 'Being seen as hit of the year after one month!'

They naturally attended the ceremony, where they were in for another surprise as the audience were all shouting their names. The band were dressed in their own unique, eye-opening style: Lene in a red spacesuit, Søren with his spikes, Claus with his bright ginger hair and René with no hair. There was no way you could fail to take notice of Aqua... or forget them!

> 'That was so way out! Being seen as hit of the year after one month!'
> RENÉ

AQUA STYLE

Together with their fresh, happy, fun-loving pop, Aqua are renowned for their wacky and colourful image. They have taken inspiration from pop acts like No Doubt, Madonna and Abba, and they got the idea for the Aqua style from the tongue-in-cheek cartoon pop of bands like Dee-Lite and the B-52s. They realized that wacky clothes and hair blended with catchy tunes was the best way to express how they felt inside.

'We'll always look and sound wild because that's what we are. We're people who love to laugh and mess around,' explains René. Unlike other bands, the Aqua style is for real – they don't dress up trying to be cool and trendy, this is how they are 24 hours a day!

Aqua don't insist that they are taken seriously, but they are serious about their music - and it shows! They love the power and energy of pop music and making it is what they're best at. They don't feel they have to always make one sort of music - they are free to do anything, be anyone!

AQUA STYLE

With her ever-changing hairstyles and wild and vivid clothes, Lene has set a new fashion trend.

'We're changing all the time, so we don't ever have one particular image,' she explains, 'and that goes for both our music and our style. People can't really understand us, in fact!'

Lene says that she didn't really change her hair when the band started out, but now she changes it all the time. One minute it's short, brown and curly, the next week it's long, falling down her back and bright red. Magazines are always

'Even our merchandise officers have told us to slow down!'

LENE

wondering what she'll do next, so that their Aqua cover shots aren't out of date!

'Even our merchandise officers have told us to slow down!' she laughs.

The Aqua image is ever-changing. Unbelievably, René is planning to grow his hair.

'I'll be wearing hats for a few months. Then... you'll have to wait and see!'

THE AQUA STORY: SCENE FIVE

CALL BARBIE A DOCTOR!

In some countries, the release of 'Barbie Girl' was the first time they'd heard of the Scandinavian quartet called Aqua, though by this time they were already on their way to stardom.

'We weren't even going to release it worldwide,' reveals Claus. 'We started playing it at radio stations and people were just screaming like crazy to hear the song. After that, the record company said we'd better release it.'

It was Søren who had the idea for the song, after visiting a kitsch exhibition in Denmark, which included Barbie dolls. He returned to the studio with the beginnings of a song about a Barbie-type person. He'd jotted down a few lyrics, which were humorous and tongue-in-cheek – and a welcome change to the usual, boring 'I love you, you love me' lyrics.

As usual, Aqua worked together to write the song: Søren and Claus came up with a tune and some lyrics, then the four sat and talked about the theme of the song. And, as usual, had a great

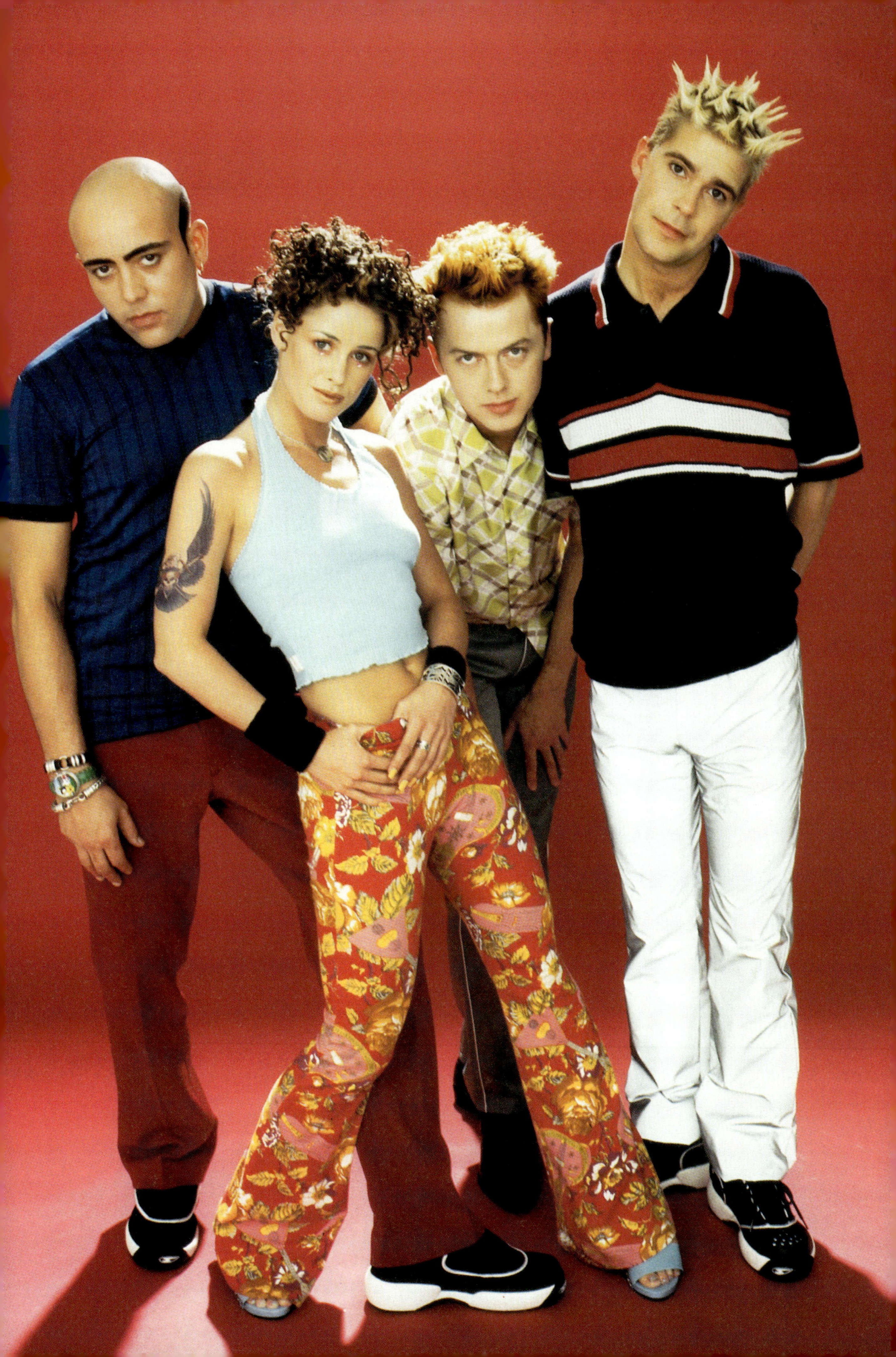

SCENE FIVE: CALL BARBIE A DOCTOR!

laugh! The song was a worldwide smash, reaching number one in 35 countries.

When Aqua first went to the USA in August 1997, they heard that Mattel, the company which makes the Barbie doll, were taking Universal Records to court over the song. The story was broadcast on the international news channel CNN; it was proving to be a very stressful time for the band and Universal.

'We couldn't understand what all the fuss was about,' reveals Claus, 'It was just a funny song. It wasn't meant to be specifically about the doll, but about people's approach to those who are a Barbie girl type of person.'

Mattel seemed to have misunderstood the humour, irony and genius that is Aqua.

The only positive thing to come out of the situation was that Aqua met lots of supportive people, including other pop stars and TV celebrities, who helped them and gave them support.

The next splash hit from Aqua was the catchy 'Doctor Jones', which again went straight into the charts at number one all over the world. In the UK over half a million people had ordered it from record shops before it had even been released!

Written by the four friends while sitting around the keyboards, it is the story of a holiday romance: Lene sings about her lost love, played by René, who is missing her just as

> 'We couldn't understand what all the fuss was about. It was just a funny song.'
> CLAUS

much. She goes to see a doctor to cure her heartbreak – it's Doctor Jones!

The band were the talk of the music world with their crazy video for the single, which took its inspiration from the Tarzan and Indiana Jones films, and featured the band lost in the jungle being spooked by voodoo and wild animals.

'It seemed like a great idea to be surrounded by all those different animals. We don't actually put too much thought into why we do things - we just do them!'

SØREN

AQUAVISION

Name	Søren Rasted
Nickname	Spike
Birthplace	Blovstrød, Denmark
Date of Birth	13 June 1969
Eye Colour	Brown
Hair Colour	Dark/Blond – it changes!
Height	6ft 2in/187cm
Weight	11st/76 kilos
Parent's Profession	Dad is an architect and mum is a homemaker
Lives	Copenhagen/London
Distinguishing Features	His laugh and spikes
Favourite Food	Desserts and free food!
Favourite Movie	Evil Dead 2
Favourite TV Show	NYPD Blue
Favourite Possession	The pot he uses for cooking soup, pasta and vegetables
Favourite Clothes	Long johns and a White Zombie T-shirt
Best Experience	When he met a Danish pop star in person after a concert in Farum
Worst Experience	Skiing off-piste at St Anton
Greatest Strength	His lack of strength
Greatest Weakness	Girls!
Education	Business College
Former Jobs	Gas station attendant and trainee accountant
Best Time of His Career	Now
Heroes and Role Models	Matt Johnson (The The)

43

THE AQUA STORY: SCENE SIX

TURN TO A DIFFERENT STYLE

Proving that Aqua are unstoppable, in the spring of 1998 'Turn Back Time' stormed into the charts to give the band a third number one, accompanied by a video filmed on London's underground.

In a way, this has been the most important number one for Aqua. People may have seen them as a funny band, which of course they are, but the soulful ballad 'Turn Back Time' reveals their more serious side, and shows how their sound can encompass different styles.

'This song shows we can do what we want to do,' says René, 'not what people expect and what is safe for us to release.'

> 'We were pleased to have our song in the film, but it wasn't written for it.'
> **LENE**

'We've been around for four years,' adds Lene, 'and we've never changed. 'Turn Back Time' isn't as crazy as 'Barbie Girl' or 'Doctor Jones' but it doesn't mean we've changed. I've still got red in my hair!'

When the band were putting *Aquarium* together, no-one really expected to hear a song like 'Turn Back Time', but Aqua wanted this track more than anything. They believed in it, though others working with them were worried because it was in a different vein to their other hits.

'It's not that important to us if other bands take us seriously or not. We just do our thing and if people think we're silly we don't care!'

'This song shows we can do what we want to do, not what people expect and what is safe for us to release.'
RENÉ

SCENE SIX: A DIFFERENT STYLE

'We just do our thing and if people think we're silly we don't care!'
LENE

'Turn Back Time' was chosen to feature in the film 'Sliding Doors' starring Gwyneth Paltrow – for many people seeing the film was the first time they heard the fantastic new tune.

'We were pleased to have our song in the film, but it wasn't written for it. They chose the song specifically,' explains Lene.

46

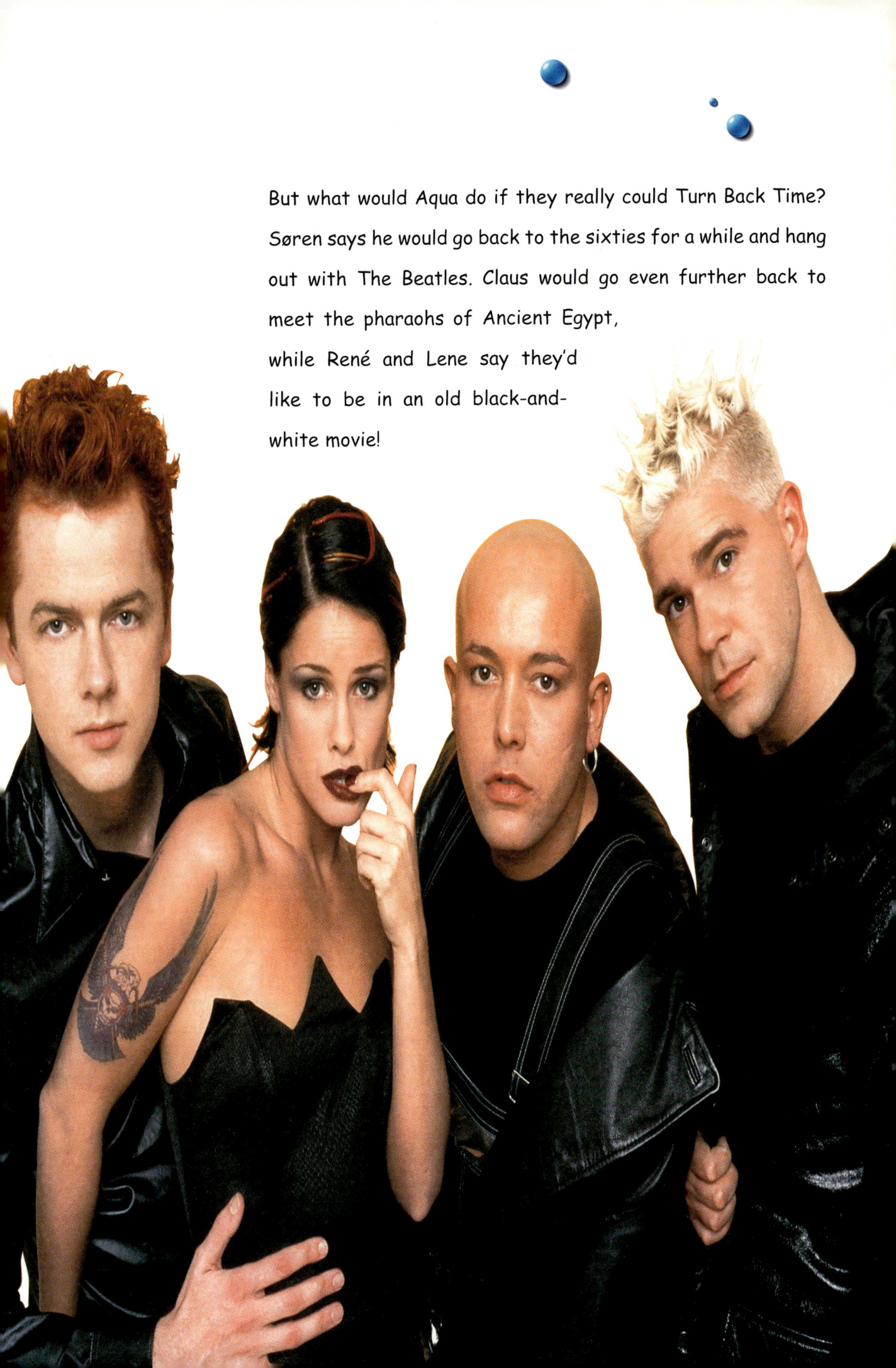

But what would Aqua do if they really could Turn Back Time? Søren says he would go back to the sixties for a while and hang out with The Beatles. Claus would go even further back to meet the pharaohs of Ancient Egypt, while René and Lene say they'd like to be in an old black-and-white movie!

ONE, TWO, THREE ACTION!

Aqua's wacky and entertaining videos have been a major aspect of their success. Unlike many videos which are only interesting the first time you see them, Aqua's videos have so much happening. Whether it's René as Doctor Jones in 'Doctor Jones', the charmer in 'Barbie Girl' and Candyman in 'Lollipop', or Lene as the Pirate Princess in 'My Oh My', each video is memorable and something you can't help but take notice of!

Made by Peter Petersson, and designed by Peter Stenbæk (who also creates the band's record sleeves), Aqua's videos are like little movies with each member playing a character. René explains: 'As they have this movie kind of theme, with intros and happy endings, there's a lot of things that you only see after you watch the videos a few times. It's like "Oh I didn't see that before."'

> 'I had these painted teeth and fake scars and René had a big wig and a wooden leg – we couldn't stop laughing!'
> **CLAUS**

Aqua's songs are like fairytales with a storyline, so the band think it's easy to make videos around them. Peter takes responsibility for illustrating the song visually: he comes up with the video theme, such as the pirate ship in 'My Oh My', puts forward his ideas and writes a script which he faxes to the band, telling them what each of their roles will be.

'We're perfectionists in everything we do, so if the script appeals to our sense of humour and irony then we'll go with it,' says Claus.

'We'll change a few things here and there, but it's usually quite straightforward,' adds René.

As the videos are always finished in less than two days, it's true to say that René, Lene, Søren and Claus are natural actors!

When it comes to Aqua's favourite video, they all agree on one: 'My Oh My'! Claus explains: "My Oh My' was really fun to make. I had these painted teeth and fake scars and René had a big wig and a wooden leg – we couldn't stop laughing!'

René adds: 'We have time to think about each storyline, then we gear ourselves up to each part. We get so excited checking out the costumes: "I want this and I want that!"'

All of Aqua's videos have been a reflection of what they are about, and what they show most of all is that these four want to have a great time!

THE AQUA STORY: SCENE SEVEN

THE FUTURE IS AQUA

For Aqua, success has been a dream come true. They have had number one records all over the world, and receive recognition and admiration wherever they go. They love what they do and stick together as friends and colleagues.

'We've never had internal problems in the band. We've stuck together and helped each other with our problems,' says Søren.

If there is one thing that Aqua love more than anything, it is the loyalty of their fans. They rarely have screaming crowds outside their hotels like boy bands do, because their fans are into them for their music and style.

'Our fans don't hassle us at all,' says Søren, 'because it's the music they want a piece of. People like us for more than just the Barbie song, they love all our songs. Barbie was a just a way into Aqua, and we've proved that.'

The thing Aqua love about performing is the energy they get from it, the kick they get from people singing their songs and wanting them to perform. As with any show, there have been things that didn't quite go to plan.

'Once we were playing at a disco in Copenhagen,' begins Lene, 'We had a huge firework filled with roses to shoot into the audience. By the time we got on stage they had swelled up with the heat. Then suddenly, in the middle of 'Roses are Red', the whole thing exploded! There was the biggest bang ever!'

'We turned around,' continues Søren, 'to see Claus lying on the floor with his keyboards on top of him!' Poor Claus had been blown over by the force of the bang!

'People like us for more than just the Barbie song, they love all our songs.'
SØREN

Luckily, this had all been caught on camera, so the image of Claus disappearing from the stage will always be with them!

There have been plenty of memories so far, such as the time in Paris when fans were grabbing hold of Lene so hard that her top came undone, and the time Søren had his trainers and trousers ripped off by fans!

'We're very close to our fans,' boasts a proud René. 'We like to play as near to them as we can. When we're about to go on stage we're always told "Don't go too near," and of course we always do!'

He adds 'We just sit there saying "Okay, okay." We give each other a little smile and then, once we're out there, we go straight to our fans!'

'The parents are so nice too,' he continues. 'They say "I don't want to bother you in your free time but I have a daughter at home and she would freak out if I got your autograph!"'

Even in countries they've never visited before, they still get butterflies in their stomach when people sing 'Doctor Jones, Jones, calling Doctor Jones...'

There have been many highlights for Aqua since they burst onto the scene, including performing on the legendary Top Of The Pops, a show on which every big name has appeared over the years.

'It's one of my favourite TV shows. It just works!' says Lene. 'It was such a big thing for us because they allowed us to do what we wanted to do. There are usually so many restrictions with television.'

The Smash Hits Tour was another highlight for Aqua – they loved touring on a bus. 'It was great, talking to all the other bands when we were rehearsing, giving each other advice and sharing problems,' explains Søren.

AQUAVISION

At the 1998 Danish Grammy Awards Aqua won:

Hit of the Year (Barbie Girl)

Pop Album of the Year

Newcomer of the Year

Video of the Year (Barbie Girl)

Band of the Year

People's Choice Award

P3 National Radio Listeners' Award

SCENE SEVEN: THE FUTURE IS AQUA

The biggest highlight so far was the Danish Grammy Awards. Aqua stole the show, walking away with six awards: four Grammys and two People's Choice Awards. According to Lene, when the name 'Aqua' was announced it was like being in a dream: 'I was in tears, I couldn't actually say thank you to anyone!'

The future certainly looks bright for Aqua. They are international stars, idolized all over the world, and wherever you go you can bet you'll hear an Aqua song! The band say they have completed the first chapter in their career and are ready to embark on the next – after they have had a good rest!

Having achieved a record-breaking three worldwide number one singles in a row, the first non-UK act ever to do this, the Scandinavian foursome struck gold again with their next single 'My Oh My'. Released in the UK in July 1998, it was the perfect soundtrack to the summer, and could be heard by the pool and on the beach all over the world.

The video to this hit is the band's favourite. Dressed as pirates sailing on the seven seas, Claus and Søren had painted-out black teeth, and René played an old man with - surprisingly - long white hair! As he says: 'This is what Aqua is all about – fun and dressing up!'

> 'This is what Aqua is all about – fun and dressing up!'
> RENÉ

After their Scandinavian tour, which kicked off on 10 July 1998, it's back to the studio to record the follow-up to the dazzling *Aquarium*, followed by a massive world tour.

'We say enjoy every day as it comes.' LENE

'We can't wait,' says an excited Søren. 'It'll be after our second album and we'll get a big band together!'

The band are clearly excited about performing on the world's largest stages, and are eager to show that as well as being one of the best pop acts around, they can also put on an amazing live show.

And after that?

'We're not really looking more than two years ahead,' says Lene, 'We say enjoy every day as it comes.'

The Aqua formula is simple. They make good pop tunes and love doing it!

LENE

AQUAVISION

Name	Lene Grawford Nystrøm
Nickname	Gullklumpen, Lemon, Baben
Birthplace	Tønsberg, Norway
Date of Birth	10 October 1973
Eye Colour	Green/Brown
Hair Colour	Mid-fair, a bit of chestnut
Height	5ft 7ins/170cm
Weight	8st 4lb/53kg
Parents' Profession	Dad works for an oil company in the North Sea. Mum is a homemaker with 1000 hobbies
Lives	Copenhagen/London
Distinguishing Features	Her smile, a big scar on her right knee and her tattoo
Favourite Food	Mexican
Favourite Movie	Ford Fairlane and science fiction movies
Favourite TV Show	No time to watch any!
Favourite Possession	Teddy bear 'Banderas', shoes and rucksack
Favourite Clothes	Anything cool and colourful
Best Experience	That's a secret
Worst Experience	Performed next to a pool and fell in singing!
Greatest Strength	Her enthusiasm, politeness and impulsive nature
Greatest Weakness	Impatience
Education	High school and guide school
Former Jobs	Bartender, model and TV host
Best Time of Her Career	Yet to come
Heroes and Role Models	Betty Boo, Marilyn Monroe, Juliette Lewis

AQUA LIVE

Whenever people see Aqua in concert, they are always surprised and impressed at how great they are live. As songwriters, people have called them the Abba of the nineties, and on stage they have been called the No Doubt of the dance world. But the thousands of fans who pack out their concerts know that Aqua are unique.

At the UK Smash Hits Pollwinner's Party, Aqua stole the show. The Grand Finale saw every performer running on to join René, Claus, Søren and Lene singing 'Barbie Girl', which was number one at the time. It was an amazing feat for a band who were relatively new to the pop world.

René says: 'It was very flattering when all the artists came running onto the stage. All of a sudden there were all these big bands watching us, thinking "What is this Aqua thing all about?"' Many of them were simply gobsmacked by this amazing, mad live act.

Aqua never ever become tired of performing their songs. Just how do they keep this fresh approach? By doing things differently every time they perform!

'When you're doing everything yourself from the start then it's up to you,' explains René. 'We always do things differently, never doing the same routine every time. We went to do a TV appearance and the interviewer said to Lene, "Where did you learn that unique way of dancing?"' This made the band laugh, because it was simply the way Lene expresses herself on stage.

'Even WE don't know what's going to happen next. We just go in and do it.'

LENE

AQUA LIVE

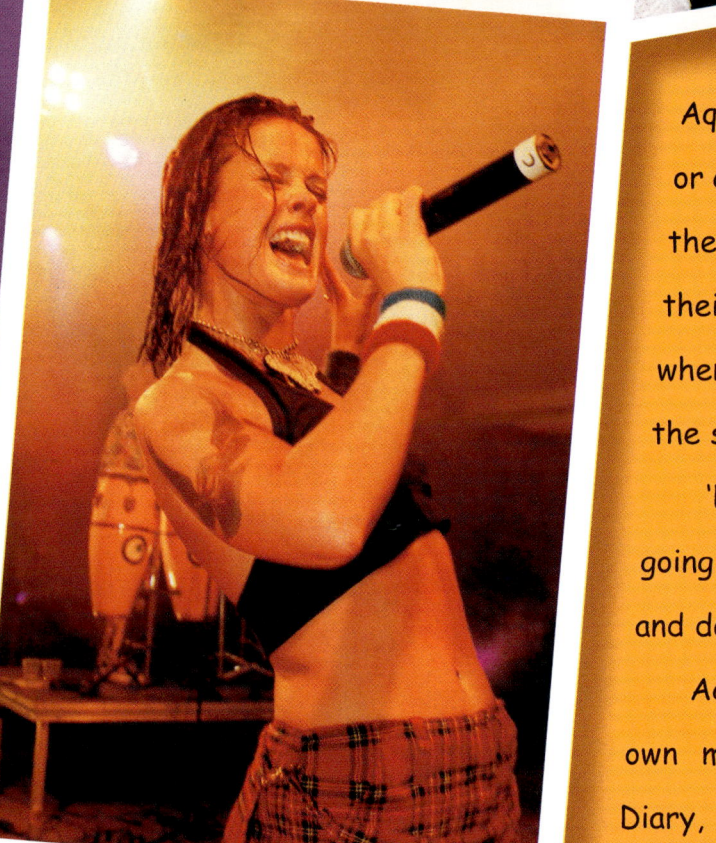

Aqua don't use trained dancers or choreographers to teach them their stage routines. They do their own thing on stage, and when they perform they never do the same thing twice.

'Even WE don't know what's going to happen next. We just go in and do it.' chuckles Lene.

Aqua have already made their own mini-documentary, The Aqua Diary, which will show even more people around the world just how great Aqua are - on the road and behind the scenes. But despite their success, René, Lene, Søren and Claus have their feet firmly on the ground.

'When you're doing everything yourself from the start then it's up to you.'
RENÉ

'We'll have to wait until we've toured and recorded our next album before we believe we are really supreme.'

Aqua have the perfect ingredients. Everyone loves pop music and everyone loves a good tune. If a tune stays in your head then that's it – and that's exactly what Aqua's songs do!

AQUA FACTS

ALBUM AWARDS AROUND THE WORLD

CANADA . . . . .9 X PLATINUM
DENMARK . . . . .7 X PLATINUM
ITALY . . . . .7 X PLATINUM
NEW ZEALAND . . . . . . .6 X PLATINUM
MALAYSIA . . . . .6 X PLATINUM
THAILAND . . . . .6 X PLATINUM
SWEDEN . . . . .5 X PLATINUM
SINGAPORE . . . . .5 X PLATINUM
NORWAY . . . . .4 X PLATINUM
HONG KONG . . . . .4 X PLATINUM
SPAIN . . . . .4 X PLATINUM
INDONESIA . . . . .4 X PLATINUM
AUSTRALIA . . . . .4 X PLATINUM
INDIA . . . . .4 X PLATINUM
PHILIPPINES . . . . .3 X PLATINUM
TAIWAN . . . . .3 X PLATINUM
USA . . . . .2 X PLATINUM
SOUTH AFRICA . . . . . .2 X PLATINUM
JAPAN . . . . .1 X PLATINUM
FINLAND . . . . .1 X PLATINUM
PORTUGAL . . . . .1 X PLATINUM
VENEZUELA . . . . .1 X PLATINUM
SWITZERLAND . . . . . .1 X PLATINUM
UNITED KINGDOM . . .1 X PLATINUM
BELGIUM . . . . .1 X PLATINUM
ARGENTINA . . . . .1 X PLATINUM
FRANCE . . . . .1 X PLATINUM
KOREA . . . . .1 X PLATINUM
POLAND . . . . .1 X PLATINUM
HOLLAND . . . . .1 X PLATINUM
CHILE . . . . .1 X PLATINUM
CZECH REPUBLIC . . . .1 X PLATINUM
AUSTRIA . . . . .1 X GOLD
GERMANY . . . . .1 X GOLD
HUNGARY . . . . .1 X GOLD
BRAZIL . . . . .1 X GOLD

Aqua have been awarded over 125 gold and platinum discs

- Aqua have been interviewed more than 2,400 times

- Aqua have been around the world 3 times

- Aqua have visited 26 different countries

- Aqua have stayed in over 110 hotels

- Aqua have sold more than 12 million albums and over 8 million singles

- Aqua have been number one in 35 countries

- Aqua have played to crowds ranging from five people in a small disco to 250,000 people on a beach in Las Palmas

- Aqua are the only international act to have made it to number one with their first three singles in the UK

- Aqua once visited four European cities in one day - interviews in Madrid, a record signing in Milan, a Top of the Pops appearance in London and finally a well-earned sleep in a hotel in Rome!

- Barbie Girl entered the Billboard Hot 100 singles chart at number seven, the highest ever for a debut hit

ACKNOWLEDGEMENTS

Thank you so much for your support, and for buying our official book. We hope you enjoy reading it!

WRITE TO AQUA AT:
THE OFFICIAL AQUA FAN CLUB
PO BOX 2019
DK 1012 COPENHAGEN K
DENMARK

AUTHOR'S ACKNOWLEDGEMENTS

Thanks to Aqua; Lene, René, Søren and Claus for their help and co-operation, John Aagaard at TG Management, Niclas Anker at Universal Music Denmark and Heather Redmond at Universal Music UK.